ADAM✦SHARP
·London Calling·

by George Edward Stanley
illustrated by Guy Francis

To all the spies in Ms. Meshew's
second-grade class at
Mattawan Early Elementary School
G.E.S.

To Calvin
G.F.

Library of Congress Cataloging-in-Publication Data
Stanley, George Edward.
Adam Sharp, London calling / by George Edward Stanley ; illustrated by
Guy Francis.
    p.   cm. — (Road to Reading. Mile 4)
Summary: Eight-year-old superspy Adam Sharp is summoned to cowboy-
infested London to find out who stole Big Ben.
ISBN 0-307-26414-9 (pbk) — ISBN 0-307-46414-8 (GB)
[1. Spies—Fiction. 2. Cowboys—Fiction. 3. London (England)—Fiction.
4. England—Fiction.] I. Francis, Guy, ill. II. Title. III. Series.

PZ7.S78693 Ab 2002
[Fic]—dc21   2001040739

A GOLDEN BOOK • NEW YORK

Text copyright © 2002 by George Edward Stanley. Illustrations
copyright © 2002 by Guy Francis. All rights reserved under
International and Pan-American Copyright Conventions. Published
in the United States by Golden Books, an imprint of Random House
Children's Books, a division of Random House, Inc., New York, and
simultaneously in Canada by Random House of Canada Limited,
Toronto. Golden Books, A Golden Book, and the G colophon are
registered trademarks of Random House, Inc.

ISBN: 0-307-26414-9 (pbk)
ISBN: 0-307-46414-8 (GB)
Printed in the United States of America   October 2002

10 9 8 7 6 5 4 3 2 1

Contents

1

Adam Drops In

"Look! Look!" said Mrs. Digby. "There's the queen!"

Adam Sharp straightened his black bow tie and joined the rest of Mrs. Digby's class in front of the TV.

Some important people in Washington, D.C., were having a parade for the queen of England.

She was sitting in a long black car and waving out the window.

"She looks like a nice person," Mrs. Digby said.

She is, Adam thought. He had met the queen many times.

That was because Adam wasn't just a student. He was also a secret agent for IM-8. IM-8 agents went on missions that were too scary for other agents.

A red light on the TV started blinking. It meant Adam was needed at IM-8 Headquarters. J would be coming to get him soon.

Everyone at Friendly Elementary

School thought J was a janitor. But J was a member of IM-8, too.

J opened Mrs. Digby's door. "The Gifted and Talented Teacher wants to see Adam Sharp," he announced.

Of course, there really wasn't a Gifted and Talented Program in Adam's school. It was just a cover for IM-8.

Adam followed J to the janitor's closet. Inside, a secret door opened into IM-8 Headquarters. T was sitting behind a big desk. T was the head of IM-8.

"The queen has a problem," T said. "She needs to see you at once, Sharp."

Adam was puzzled. "But isn't the queen in a parade?" he asked.

T nodded. "You'll have to parachute through the sunroof of her car."

"Good idea, sir," Adam said.

The IM-8 helicopter was parked on the roof of the school. T and Adam climbed inside and lifted off.

The helicopter passed over Adam's neighborhood. "Look, T! There's my new tree house!" Adam shouted. "Dad and I just finished building it!"

"Impressive!" said T.

Washington, D.C., wasn't far from Friendly, Maryland, so it didn't take long to get there.

"I see the parade!" Adam told T. "There's the queen's car!"

"Get ready, Sharp!" T said. "Unzip your backpack!"

Adam did as he was instructed.

The helicopter flew over the long black car. Adam could see the sunroof.

It was small, but Adam was sure he
could make it.

He was very good at what he did.

"Now!" T shouted. Adam jumped
from the helicopter. A parachute
popped out of his backpack.

Adam drifted down toward the car. He moved the cords back and forth to hit his target. He slipped through the sunroof and landed in a seat right beside the queen. Quickly, he pulled the parachute in after him.

"Good morning, Sharp. I've been expecting you to drop in." The queen whistled. "Nice tuxedo!"

"Thank you, Your Majesty," Adam said. He wore a tuxedo every day. "So what can IM-8 do for you?"

"No one in London woke up on time this morning," the queen said. "Somebody stole Big Ben!"

2

Do-Si-Do

"Big Ben!" Adam exclaimed. "That's the most famous clock in the world!"

"Quite right," the queen said. "Now there's just a big hole where Big Ben used to be!"

"Have you talked to MI-5, MI-6, and MI-7?" Adam asked. "Your spies are good."

"I've asked them, Sharp. They don't know a thing," the queen said. "And no one can compare to IM-8."

Adam's heart swelled with pride. "We are the best, Your Majesty," he said. "We'll solve this problem for you."

The queen's car pulled up to the White House. "I can't stay in the U.S. long," the queen said. "I must get back to the palace right away."

"I'll be in touch, Your Majesty."

Adam gave the president a quick wave, then raced across the south lawn. T was waiting for him. They flew to Friendly Airport and traded the

9

IM-8 helicopter for the IM-8 jet.

"Who's our contact in London?" Adam asked.

"Magna Carter," T replied.

Adam radioed Magna. He told her what the queen had said.

Magna yawned. "Hullo! I didn't wake up on time, either. I was late for math lessons. And, Adam, something else is going on here. Cowboys and cowgirls are everywhere!"

"Hmmm. That is strange. I'll be in London in five hours, Magna," Adam said. "See what else you can find out."

"Right-o!" Magna said. "Cheerio!"

Just as Adam was closing his eyes to take a nap, the queen's jet roared past.

Magna met Adam at the airport. She was wearing a red minidress and white go-go boots. In her hand, she held a clear plastic umbrella.

"Is it raining?" Adam asked.

"Gosh no," Magna said. "But in London, you never know when an umbrella will come in handy."

They found a taxi and took it to the Houses of Parliament. Magna pointed out where Big Ben used to be.

"This is worse than I imagined," Adam said. He stopped and listened. "What's that noise?"

"Blimey!" Magna said. "It's coming from the Chamber of the House of Lords!"

They ran to the Chamber. Inside, cowboys and cowgirls were square dancing. All the lords clapped along.

"We need to talk to these cowboys and cowgirls, Magna," Adam said. "They may know something about Big Ben."

Adam and Magna linked arms with the dancers. The square-dance caller said, "Twirl your partner so she'll glide. Men to the middle, women outside."

"Men to the middle!" the dancers repeated. "Women outside!"

Adam went with the men to the middle of the square. Magna joined the women on the outside. Adam and Magna passed each other and stopped in front of different partners.

Great! Adam thought. *Now I'll find*

out what's going on. "Excuse me. I'm looking for the person who stole Big Ben," he said to a cowgirl.

"Allemande left!" the cowgirl yelled.

"He did?" Adam said. "Where did he go?"

All of a sudden, another cowgirl was in front of Adam. "Howdy!" she shouted.

"Howdy!" Adam said. He grabbed her hand and twirled her around. "Who stole Big Ben?" he asked.

"Sashay to your right!" the cowgirl whooped.

Adam turned to the cowgirl on his right. "You mean *her*?" he said. "*She stole Big Ben?*"

But when he turned back around, his partner was gone, and Magna was standing in front of him. "Did you find out who stole Big Ben?" she asked.

"No. These cowgirls are talking in secret code, Magna," Adam said.

"Let's check the IM-8 code book,"

Magna said. "But first I have to call my mum. I need to tell her I won't be home for supper."

"Good idea," Adam said.

It had started to rain, so Adam and Magna both crowded into a telephone booth. Just as Magna was dialing, the booth shook.

Adam looked through the glass door. "Magna!" he cried. "A wrecker truck is picking us up with its crane!"

The telephone booth dangled from the crane hook behind the truck. The driver gunned the motor and took off.

"Hold on, Magna!" Adam shouted.

The wrecker truck raced through London. The red telephone booth swung wildly back and forth. Adam and Magna watched helplessly as buildings whizzed by.

Finally, the truck stopped at the Thames River. Adam saw a huge ship with the words *SS Houston* on its side. *Hmmm,* Adam thought. *Houston is a city in Texas. And in Texas, there are lots of cowboys, too.*

The wrecker truck dropped the telephone booth onto the deck of the ship. The deck was covered with hundreds of other telephone booths.

"They're stealing all our little red
telephone booths!" Magna cried.

Adam pushed the door open. The
deckhands were too busy running
around the ship to notice them. "I have
an idea, Magna," he said. "Follow me."

They ran from telephone booth to

telephone booth. At the end of the deck, they reached a door that said *PRIVATE! KEEP OUT!*

Adam whispered, "I think we'll find what we're looking for in here." He turned the knob and slipped inside.

It was a small office. It had a desk, a telephone, and a filing cabinet. Adam went to the filing cabinet. He found the

file he wanted. It said *SHIPOWNER*.

Adam quickly read the file. "This is it!" He picked up the telephone. He dialed the queen's number.

"Hullo," the queen said.

"Your Majesty! Sharp here!" Adam said. "I know who stole Big Ben! His name is Big Bubba. He's also stealing all the little red telephone booths."

"Forget Big Ben, Sharp. Forget the telephone booths, too," the queen sobbed. "Big Bubba is standing right here. He's going to take Buckingham Palace!"

3

Hog-tied

Adam and Magna raced off the ship.
A taxi was just pulling away from the
docks. They jumped inside.

The taxi couldn't go fast because the
streets were packed with cows. Finally,
it arrived at Buckingham Palace.

A tall, skinny cowboy stood at the
front door. There was a rattlesnake

coiled around his ten-gallon hat. The cowboy was pointing to a long piece of paper and arguing with the queen.

"That must be Big Bubba!" Adam said. He and Magna ran to the front door of the palace. They had to dodge several bulls on their way.

"Thank goodness you're here," the queen sobbed. She blew her nose on a pretty purple handkerchief. "Please meet Mr. Big Bubba. He's from Texas."

"What's going on?" Adam asked.

"Me and my cowboys are movin' Buckingham Palace to Texas," Big Bubba replied.

"Blimey!" Magna cried. "Where will the queen live?"

Big Bubba shrugged.

Maybe she could live in my new tree house, Adam thought. He'd talk to her about it later.

"Is Texas where you took Big Ben?" Adam asked.

"Yep," Big Bubba said. "But Big Ben has a new name. It's called Big Bubba."

The queen gasped. She looked faint. "Big *Bubba*?" she said.

Adam turned to the queen. "How could this happen, Your Majesty?"

"My great-great-grandmother

signed a secret agreement with Texas in 1845," the queen said. "It was so secret nobody knew about it."

"What does it say?" Magna asked.

"It gives England to Texas," the queen replied.

Big Bubba waved the paper. "That's right! It all goes! Yee-ha!"

"This is terrible, Your Majesty!" Adam said. "What will the people of England think?"

"A lot of them are excited, Sharp," the queen said. "They want to be cowboys and cowgirls."

Just then, Adam noticed that the queen was wearing cowgirl boots. He didn't mention it.

There has to be something I can do, Adam thought. "Let me see that," he said.

Big Bubba handed Adam the long piece of paper. Adam looked at it carefully. It was hard to read. There were black smudges all over it.

"This is a copy!" Adam said.

"Of course it's a copy, Sharp!" the queen said. "All of our *real* secret documents are kept in a safe in the Tower of London."

"Then that's where we need to go, Magna!" Adam said.

"Hold on, pardner! I can't let you do that!" Big Bubba said. His lasso looped through the air. Seconds later, he had hog-tied Adam, Magna, and the queen to the throne. "This'll teach you not to mess with Big Bubba!"

Big Bubba ran out the front door of

the palace and jumped onto his horse.

"We need to cut through this lasso, Your Majesty," Adam said. "Where do you keep the Royal Knives?"

"In the Royal Knife Drawer," the queen told him. "Unfortunately, that's in the Royal Kitchen."

"Rats!" Adam said.

"Don't get your knickers in a twist, Sharp!" Magna said.

Adam turned red. "My knickers are fine!"

"No! No! That means calm down," Magna said. "We don't need a knife!" She wiggled her go-go boots in the air.

"These boots aren't just for walking!"
Magna clicked her heels together.
Out popped two mini buzz saws.
Quickly, Magna sawed through the
ropes. In minutes, they were free.

"May we borrow the Royal Car,
Your Majesty?" Adam asked.

"Sorry, Sharp. It's full of hay for Big Bubba's horse," the queen said. "But the Royal Coach isn't being used."

"We'll take that!" Adam said.

The queen rang for the coachman and the footmen. Adam and Magna climbed inside the Royal Coach.

The queen showed them how to wave to the people. Then she handed Magna a map of the Tower of London. "The Keeper of the Secrets has the key to the safe," she whispered.

"Where to?" the coachman asked.

"The Tower of London!" Adam shouted.

4

The Bloody Tower

The Royal Coach raced through London. Adam and Magna waved to the people, just as the queen had taught them.

The people waved back.

"Blimey!" Magna said. "I feel like Cinderella!"

The coach pulled up to the Tower of

London. The footmen opened the doors. Adam and Magna jumped out.

"Wow! This place is huge!" Adam said. "Which tower do we go to?"

"The *Bloody* Tower," Magna said. "That's where the safe is on the map."

They headed to the Bloody Tower. Along the way, they passed several signs: *Henry VI died here in 1471. Anne Boleyn died here in 1536. Sir Walter Raleigh died here in 1618.*

Adam shivered.

He hoped they wouldn't have to put up a sign about him.

They reached the Bloody Tower and

went inside. They climbed up a narrow stone stairway.

Suddenly, a knight in armor jumped out. "Heh! Heh! Heh!" he said.

"It's my archenemy, General Menace!" Adam shouted. "I'd know that laugh anywhere."

General Menace took off his helmet.
"Well, well, well! Adam Sharp and
Magna Carter," he said. "What can I do
for you?"

"Nothing!" Adam looked around.
"Where's the Keeper of the Secrets?"

"At your service, Sharp!" General
Menace said. "Heh! Heh! Heh!"

"*You?*" Magna gasped.

"I should have known you'd be
behind this evil plan!" Adam said.
"Hand over the key to the safe,
General Menace!"

"The secret document you want isn't
in the safe, Sharp. It's behind that big

block of wood over there," General Menace said. "But you'll have to get down on your knees and lean over to reach it. Heh! Heh! Heh!"

Adam walked over to the big block of wood.

He knelt down.

He leaned over.

"This will be easy," Adam said. "There's even a place to put my neck."

General Menace picked up an ax.

"Adam! Watch out!" Magna cried. "You just put your head on the chopping block!"

5

Adam Saves the Queen

Adam grabbed the ax with his right
hand and the secret document with his
left hand.

"I knew what you were planning to
do all along, General Menace!" he said.
"You can't outsmart IM-8!"

"He's right, General Menace!" said
Magna. She pointed her umbrella at

him and pushed a button. A dueling
sword popped out.

"Hey! That's not fair!" General
Menace cried. "I don't have a sword."

"Right-o," Magna said. "Sorry." She
punched another button. The sword
slid back into the umbrella.

Right away, General Menace pulled

out a sword from behind his back. "Gotcha!" he said. "Heh! Heh! Heh!"

"You lied!" Magna said. She conked General Menace on the head with the umbrella, and he clanged to the floor.

"Look, Magna!" Adam cried. He was reading the *real* secret document. "There's something strange here!"

Magna looked. "Blimey! This isn't the deed to ENGLAND! This is the deed to FENGLAND!"

"What's 'Fengland'?" Adam asked.

"Fengland was a small island," Magna explained. "In the 1800s, it was a colony of England."

Adam studied the secret document. "General Menace must have erased the *F* on the copy he gave Big Bubba!"

"That changes everything!" Magna said. "Fengland sank in 1872. This document is worthless!"

"O-o-o-o-h! O-o-o-o-h!"

Adam and Magna turned. General Menace was waking up.

"Why did you erase the *F*, General Menace?" Adam asked.

"I wanted my own island. England was the perfect place for my new headquarters," General Menace said. "I made a deal with Big Bubba. He'd

take the buildings. I'd take the land."

"That is so evil!" Magna said.

"And I almost got away with it, too!" General Menace said. "I was about to burn the queen's *real* secret document when you showed up." He snarled at Adam. "I'll get you next time, Sharp. You'll never foil my plans again!"

"There will be no next time," Adam said. "I'm taking you in."

Suddenly, the room filled with
smoke. It smelled like barbecued
chicken. Adam couldn't see a thing.

"Come on, pardner! I'm bustin' you
out of here!" It was Big Bubba!

"Heh! Heh! Heh!" General Menace
said. "See you later, Sharp!"

When the smoke cleared, General Menace was gone.

Adam and Magna took the Royal Coach back to the palace. The queen met them at the door.

"We found the *real* secret document, Your Majesty," Adam said. "England doesn't belong to Texas after all." He told the queen what it *really* said. "And Big Ben will be returned."

"Thank you, Sharp! Thank you, Carter!" the queen said. "IM-8 has saved my kingdom! How can I ever repay you?"

Adam remembered how much Mrs. Digby liked the queen. "Could you come to my school for show-and-tell?" he asked.

"Blimey, Adam! That would blow our cover!" Magna cried. "Normal kids don't know the queen."

Oh yeah, Adam thought. He'd forgotten. "Spying is a tough job, Your Majesty," he said. "You can't use any of the good stuff for show-and-tell."

The queen smiled. "Well, how about a cup of tea instead?"

"Right-o!" Adam said.